Story by Alex de Campi
Art by Federica Manfredi

HAMBURG // LONDON // LOS ANGELES // TOKYO

visit us at www.abdopublishing.com

Reinforced library bound edition published in 2009 by Spotlight, a division of ABDO Publishing Group, 8000 West 78th Street, Edina, Minnesota 55439. This edition reprinted by arrangement with TOKYOPOP Inc. www.tokyopop.com

Written by	Alex de Campi
Illustrated by	Federica Manfredi
Tones	Cari Corene
Lettering	Lucas Rivera
Development Editor	Carol Fox
Cover Design	Jose Macasocol Jr. & Federica Manfredi
Editor	Tim Beedle
Digital Imaging Manager	Chris Buford

Library of Congress Cataloging-in-Publication Data

De Campi, Alex.

Kat & Mouse / story by Alex de Campi ; art by Federica Manfredi. -- Reinforced library bound ed.

v. cm.

Summary: Collects three previously published manga volumes in which classmates Kat Foster and Mee-Seen "Mouse" Huang investigate events involving their private school, Dover Academy, and a mysterious thief known as the Artful Dodger.

Contents: Teacher torture -- Tripped -- The ice storm.

ISBN 978-1-59961-566-0 (vol. 3: The ice storm : alk. paper)

1. Graphic novels. [1. Graphic novels. 2. Schools--Fiction. 3. Friendship--Fiction. 4. Robbers and outlaws--Fiction. 5. Mystery and detective stories.] I. Manfredi, Federica, ill. II. Title. III. Title: Kat and Mouse.

PZ7.7.D32Kat 2009

[Fic]--dc22 2008002189

All Spotlight books have reinforced library binding and are manufactured in the United States of America.

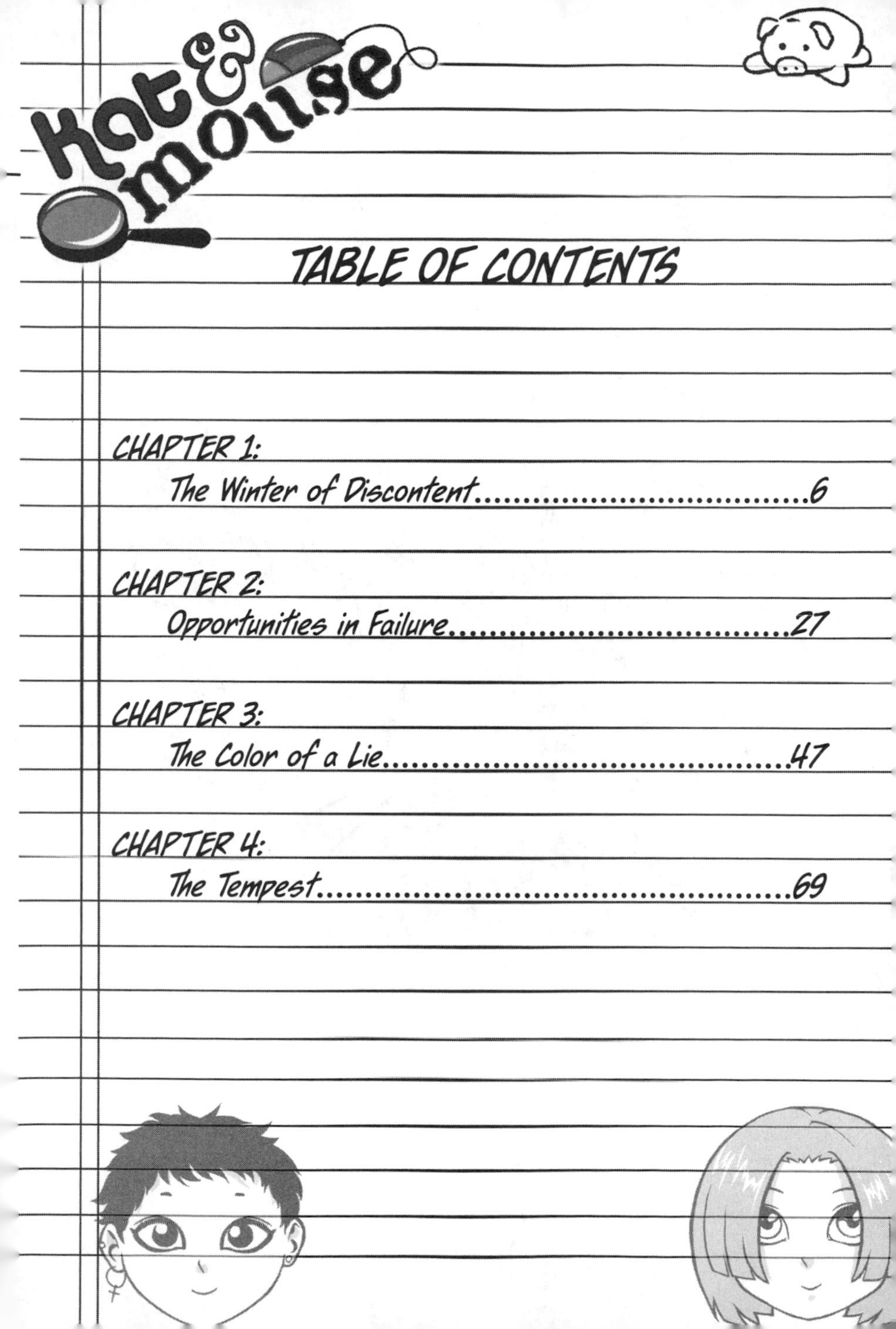

TABLE OF CONTENTS

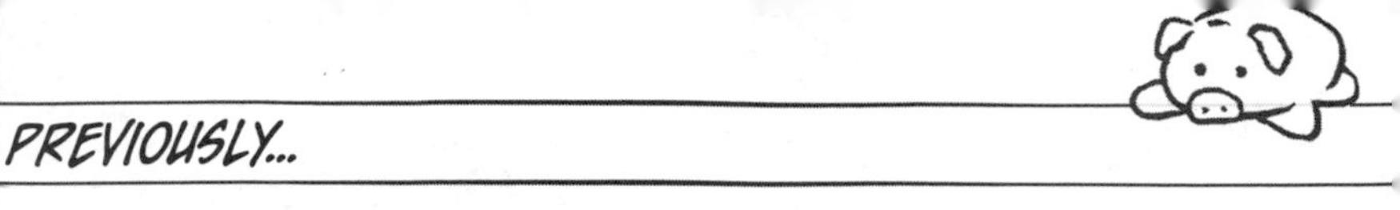

PREVIOUSLY...

When her father accepts a new job teaching science at a prestigious private school in New Hampshire, Kat Foster has no choice but to pack up her things and move with her family to Dover—a wealthy community where they don't exactly fit in. Kat quickly falls to the bottom of the social ladder at her school, but she does make one new friend: Mee-Seen Huang. Mee-Seen—or "Mouse" as she prefers to be known—is a punky skateboarder who takes pride in the fact that she stands out. Kat's also made a few rivals, notably the "Chloettes," a frequently snobby trio of princesses.

Kat and Mouse have faced many challenges at Dover Academy, most of which are caused by The Artful Dodger—a mysterious thief who has been stealing valuables around campus. Kat and Mouse have vowed to bring the thief to justice. However, despite their best efforts, the identity of The Artful Dodger remains a mystery.

Chapter 1:
The Winter of Discontent

SCIENCE
CLASSROOM
DOVER
7° GRADE SCIENCE
Unit test
Mouse Huang
TAP
TAP

GO DOVER! BEAT ST. PETER'S!
IT'S OFFICIAL: I'M DYING OF FROSTBITE.
UH-HUH.
reserved
TAP TAP TAP

DOVER ACADEMY
ST. PETER'S ACADEMY
HOME
45:00
VISITOR
00
00
11

A GIANT METEOR IS HURTLING TOWARDS EARTH. WE HAVE SEVEN MINUTES TO LIVE.
COOL.
reserved
HMPH.
OOH, LOOK!
THE GAME'S ABOUT TO STAR--
TOUCH
AAAAAGH!

Unit
Mouse Huang
A
by the sun?
YOUR HANDS ARE FREEZING!
I SWEAR YOU HAVE FROSTBITE.
reserved
ENCE
Unit test
Ollie Kim
HEY, NICK, I HEARD YOUR PARENTS WERE COMING TO THE GAME.

GUESS US MAKING IT TO THE FINALS GOT THEIR ATTENTION, HUH?
YEAH, GUESS SO.
I SAVED THEM SOME PRIMO SEATS RIGHT OVER THERE...
reserved
7° GR
Unit test
Ollie Kim
ted by the sun?
ergy?
EXCELLENT! SO THEY CAN WATCH *ME* SCORE THE WINNING GOAL!
YEAH, OLLIE!
UNLESS *I* SCORE IT FIRST.
DOVE
7° GRADE
Unit test
Ruth Applebaum
HMM...

Unit tes
B
Ruth Applebaum
d by the sun?
SORRY I'M LATE!
GRUMBLE
THE SNOW BALL COMMITTEE MEETING WAS, LIKE, E-TER-NAL.
WHAT THEME DID THEY PICK?
OH MY GOSH, YOU SO HAVE TO SPILL!
I'M NOT SUPPOSED TO TELL...

...BUT IT'S "HEAVEN ON EARTH"!
I WONDER IF THEY REALIZE THE INHERENT IRONY IN THAT.
UGH.

I THOUGHT WE COULD GO AS THREE ANGELS!
WE COULD JUST NOT GO, Y'KNOW.

WE COULD BIKE INTO TOWN AND SEE A MOVIE AT THE IOKA! AND THEN WE COULD GO FOR PIZZA AND IT WOULD BE TOTALLY--

...

SIGH... THIS IS WHAT I HATE ABOUT SCHOOL DANCES.
IF WE GO, WE'LL FEEL LIKE LOSERS.
AND IF WE DON'T GO, WE'LL FEEL LIKE LOSERS.
SIGH...
OKAY, WE'LL GO.
DOVER ACADEMY
ST. PETER'S ACADEMY
HOME
VISITOR
40:07
00
00
HI, DAD! HI, MOM!

DID WE MISS ANYTHING?
NOPE! THE GAME IS STILL ZERO-ZERO.
DOVE ACADEMY
MORE IMPORTANTLY, HOW DID THE SCIENCE TEST GO TODAY?
OH, I ACED IT.
YOU DID?
IT'S ALL COOL. PETER GAVE ME THE ANSWERS.
GOOD, BECAUSE I'M SERIOUS ABOUT GROUNDING YOU FROM THE SNOW BALL UNLESS YOU START PASSING SCIENCE.
DOVE ACADEMY

PETER?!
THAT PETER?
HE GOT THE ANSWERS OFF THE INTERNET, OR SOMETHING.
DUDE, WATCH IT! WE CAN'T AFFORD A FOUL.
SHUT UP. NOBODY SAW.
GUESS YOUR FOLKS BLEW YOU OFF AGAIN, HUH?
PARKMAN
reserved
NICE ONE, BONEHEAD.
SMACK

Sigh...

DOVER ACADEMY
7° GRADE SCIENCE
Unit test
F
Peter Parkman

7° GRADE SCIENCE
Unit test
F
Peter Parkman
FLAP

chK

LAST ONE.

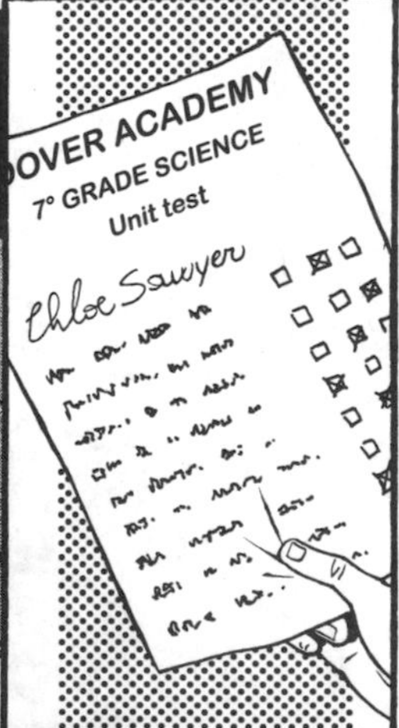
DOVER ACADEMY
7° GRADE SCIENCE
Unit test
Chloe Sawyer

DOVER ACADEMY
ST. PETER'S ACADEMY
HOME
VISITOR
0:59
00
00

DOVER ACADEMY

YEAH! GO, OLLIE!
AAAGH!

WHAT?
YOUR HANDS ARE *STILL* FREEZING!

AND SINCE WHEN DID YOU CARE ABOUT SOCCER?
SINCE IT GOT US OUT OF FIELD HOCKEY PRACTICE.
I MEAN, WHO WOULD INVENT A SPORT THAT DELIBERATELY ARMS POPULAR GIRLS WITH BIG STICKS?
CLEARLY, A POPULAR GIRL.
reserved
LOOK! OLLIE'S SETTING NICK UP TO SCORE!

YAY! GO, NICK!
YAAAY!
HMM?
brrrt brrrt
DOW

TARKINGTON
10
T. PETER'S
ACADEMY
VISITOR
00

YEAH!
GO NICK!
DOVER ACADEMY
HOME
ACADEMY
VISITOR
GO!

GO YEAH! NICK!
reserved

DOVER ACADEMY
ST. PETE
ACADEMY
HOME
0:06
VISITOR
00
00
TARKINGTON
10
reserved
AAH!
SMACK!

MM-HMM. I SEE.
ACA
BZZZZT!
NICK!
NO.
THAT WAS YOUR SCIENCE TEACHER ON THE PHONE.
YOU'RE NOT GOING ANYWHERE, YOUNG LADY.

Chapter 2:
Opportunities in Failure
PHYSICS
CHLO
EXERCISE BOOK

WELL, THAT WAS WEIRD.

WAS YOUR OLD SCHOOL THIS WEIRD?
I MEAN, I WENT TO SCHOOL IN THE BRONX AND MY OLD SCHOOL WASN'T THIS WEIRD.
WELL, WE DIDN'T HAVE A SCHOOL THIEF WHO'S A CHARLES DICKENS FAN, OR MYSTERIOUS HOT ART TEACHERS, OR EUROPEAN PRINCESSES, OR THE CLASS SOCCER STAR THROWING THE FINAL GAME OF THE SEASON, OR KIDS HOLDING TEACHERS RANSOM...
BUT SPENCER HAD ITS WEIRD MOMENTS.
We had cow tipping.
HUH. I WONDER WHAT THE NORMAL SCHOOLS ARE LIKE?
MAYBE NOWHERE IS NORMAL.
MAYBE NORMAL ONLY EXISTS IN BOOKS.

SEE YA TOMORROW.
OH!
WHAT DRESS ARE YOU GONNA WEAR TO THE DANCE?
DRESS?
THE SNOW BALL'S A FORMAL.
YOU KNOW. SHINY, EXPENSIVE INSTRUMENT OF SOCIAL HUMILIATION?

WHAT ARE YOU STANDING OUT HERE FOR?
HUH?
IT'S FREEZING.
COME ON IN. I'VE JUST MADE HOT CHOCOLATE.
UH-OH! HERE IT COMES!

THE CRASH, FLOP AND SIGH OF A BAD DAY AT SCHOOL!
CRASH!
FLOP
Sigh!
IT WASN'T *THAT* BAD...

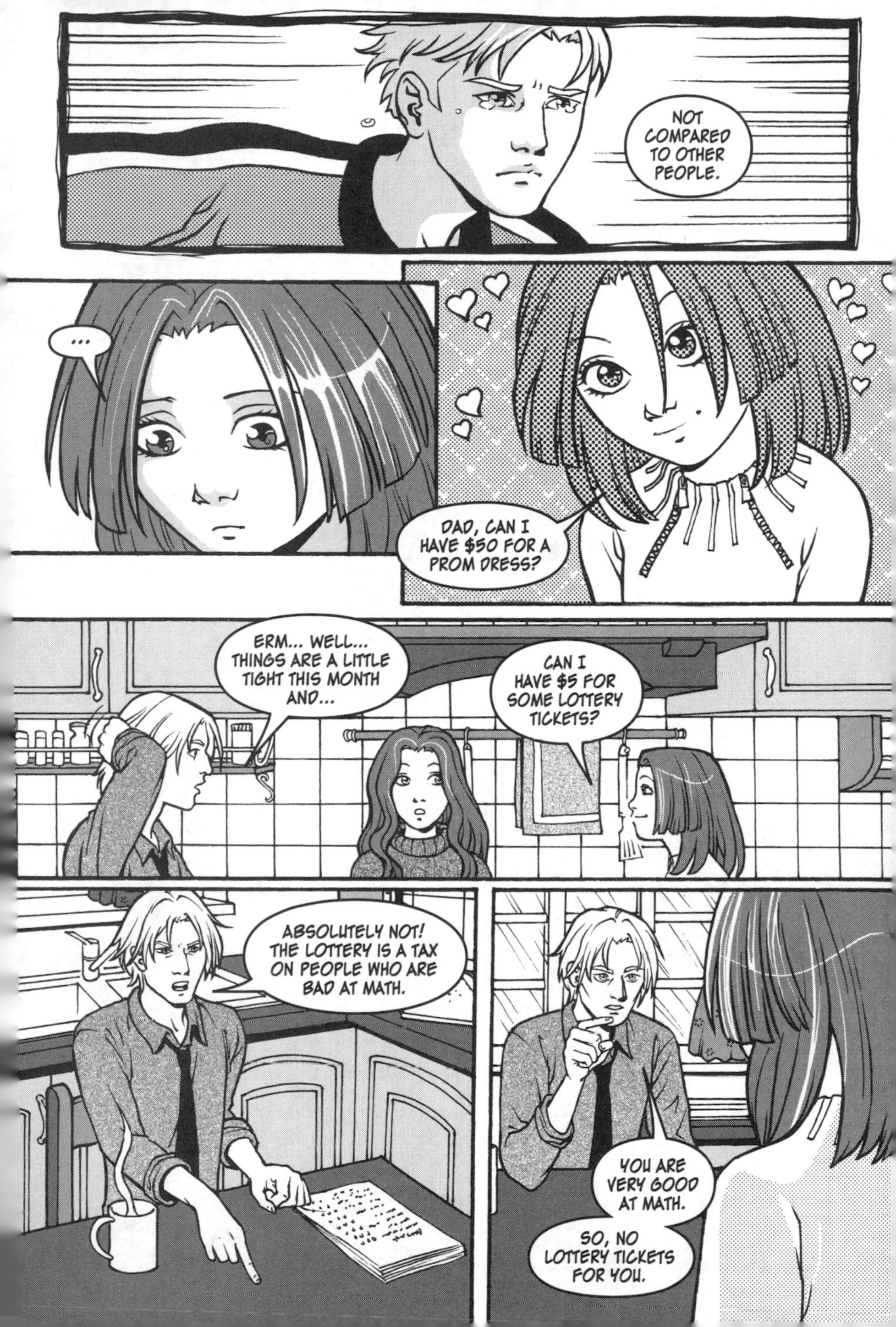
NOT COMPARED TO OTHER PEOPLE.
...
DAD, CAN I HAVE $50 FOR A PROM DRESS?
ERM... WELL... THINGS ARE A LITTLE TIGHT THIS MONTH AND...
CAN I HAVE $5 FOR SOME LOTTERY TICKETS?
ABSOLUTELY NOT! THE LOTTERY IS A TAX ON PEOPLE WHO ARE BAD AT MATH.
YOU ARE VERY GOOD AT MATH.
SO, NO LOTTERY TICKETS FOR YOU.

BUT LET ME USE MY MAGIC POWERS OF DAD-NESS ON YOUR PROBLEM.
HMMMMM...
CAN I JUST SAY THAT, MUCH AS I LOVE YOU, IF YOU EVER DO THAT IN PUBLIC, I WILL RUN AWAY TO NEW YORK CITY AND BEGIN A LIFE OF DEGRADATION ON THE STREETS?
MMMM?
EVEN IF I KNOW A SURE-FIRE WAY FOR YOU TO EARN $50 BEFORE THE DANCE?
REALLY?!

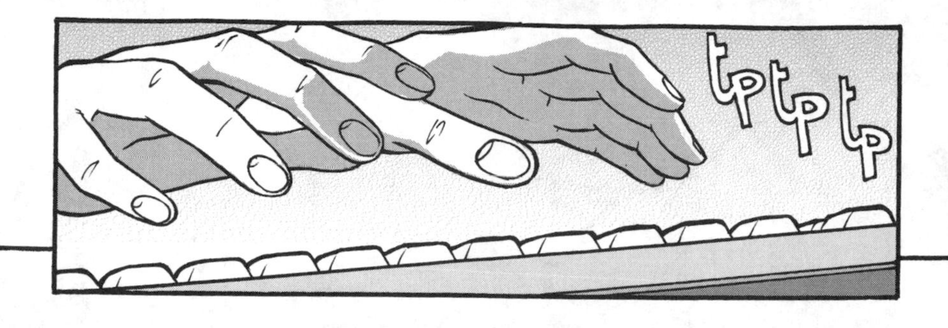

MOUSETHATROARED

KATGIRL: So there are 2 kids that need to get an A on the next science quiz or they'll get grounded and can't go to the dance

MOUSETHATROARED: Who who who?

KATGIRL: And Dad says their parents will pay for tutoring

MOUSETHATROARED: TELL already

KATGIRL: Well... one's Chloe

MOUSETHATROARED: Ew.

KATGIRL: The other's Peter

MOUSETHATROARED: EW!!!

MOUSETHATROARED: I have a can of disinfectant, if you need it

KATGIRL: LOL! No I can only tutor one

KATGIRL: I only have 2 weeks left to find out who the school thief is

KATGIRL: If the Artful Dodger is stealing stuff to scare off Princess Marie-Louise from going to Dover, then I bet he or she's got something really big planned

KATGIRL: Plus, oh yeah, my own homework

MOUSETHATROARED: So who's the lucky jerk, then?

▽BUDDIES 1/10

Mousethatroared
Leeanne123
Micaela
Jimmy
...

▷FAMILY 1/3

▷COLLEGUES

SEND

WHOA.
BING
BING

HEY.
HEY.
THANKS FOR SAYING YOU'LL TUTOR ME...
...BUT YOU'RE KINDA WASTING YOUR TIME.
IT WOULD TAKE A MIRACLE FOR ME TO UNDERSTAND WHAT'S GOING ON IN SCIENCE CLASS.
ISN'T CHRISTMAS THE SEASON OF MIRACLES?

THE QUIZ IS MAINLY GOING TO BE ABOUT EYES AND HOW WE SEE, SO WE'LL START OFF REVIEWING THE WAY LIGHT INTERACTS WITH STUFF.
SO CAN YOU EXPLAIN WHAT THE DIFFERENCE BETWEEN REFLECTION, REFRACTION AND ABSORPTION IS?
UH...
DO YOU WANT SOME BROWNIES?
THE COOK JUST MADE THESE REALLY EXCELLENT ONES! I'LL JUST--
NOPE.

I'M NOT GOING TO ESCAPE, AM I?
NOPE.
DEATH BY SCIENCE, I'M AFRAID.
BUT IF YOU BRING ME A GLASS OF WATER, I CAN SHOW YOU AN EASY WAY TO UNDERSTAND REFRACTION.
OKAY. WATER.
AND BROWNIES. I NEED SUGAR TO GET THROUGH THIS.

MUNCH
MUNCH
SO WHY DOES IT DO THAT?
WELL... YOU EVER TRIED TO RUN IN A SWIMMING POOL?
UH-HUH.
IT'S A LOT TOUGHER THAN RUNNING ON LAND, ISN'T IT?
IT'S LIKE THAT FOR THE LIGHT WAVES GOING THROUGH THE WATER.
THEY CAN STILL PASS THROUGH IT, BECAUSE IT'S TRANSPARENT. BUT IT'S HARDER.
SO THE LIGHT GETS SLOWED DOWN, AND THAT'S WHAT MAKES THE PENCIL LOOK BENT TO US.
FREAKY COOL.

REFRACTION IS HOW PRISMS WORK, TOO. THEY SLOW DOWN THE SEVEN COLORS THAT MAKE UP WHITE LIGHT AT DIFFERENT SPEEDS.
RED LIGHT IS STRONGER THAN BLUE LIGHT, SO IT DOESN'T GET BENT AS MUCH WHEN IT PASSES THROUGH THE PRISM.
OKAY, I'M CONFUSED AGAIN.
In art class, if you mix all the colors together, you get this fugly brown.
WELL, LIGHT'S SPECIAL.
SEE, THAT LIGHT BULB LOOKS WHITE, BUT WHEN IT REFLECTS IN THIS CD, IT BECOMES A RAINBOW.
It's not the same as prism refraction, but it's close enough.
OOH! I HAVE SOMETHING THAT COULD WORK AS A PRISM!

WAIT A SEC.
rustle rustle

YAAAH!
I SAID I'D BE HOME BY 6:30!
GOT IT!

TA-DAH!
IT'S MY MOM'S, BUT SHE'S LETTING ME BORROW IT.
WHOA... REAL DIAMONDS.
UH...
Wow, they DO make rainbow sparkles.
CHLOE, I'M REALLY LATE FOR DINNER.
I GOTTA GO, OR MY MOM WILL KILL ME.

HANKS FOR TUTORING ME. I THINK I ACTUALLY GET SOME OF THIS STUFF NOW.
NO PROBLEM. IT'S BEEN...MORE FUN THAN I THOUGHT.
CHLOE'S PRETTY NICE ON HER OWN.
SEE YOU TOMORROW.
YEAH, SEE Y--
DUH!
I LEFT MY BAG UPSTAIRS.

CHLOE...?

AAAAH!

Chapter 3:
The Color of a Lie

DOVER ACADEMY
THE SCHOOL THIEF?!
KLIK

ARE YOU OKAY?
YEAH.
I JUST TRIPPED.
IN THE DARK.
I'M FINE NOW. SEE YOU AT SCHOOL.

SO YOU THINK CHLOE HAD SOMETHING TO DO WITH THE ROBBERIES?

I DON'T KNOW...
I HAD ASSUMED THE THIEF WORKED ALONE.
BUT NOW...

...THE MYSTERY DEEPENS.
SNIF SNIF

THAT AIN'T THE ONLY MYSTERY.

HEY, NERD. WHY YOU TUTORING HER, BUT NOT ME?
MAYBE BECAUSE CHLOE NEVER TRIED TO PUNCH HER.
BECAUSE YOUR DAD'S FAILING ME IN SCIENCE, I CAN'T GO TO THE SNOW BALL!
WHAT AM I SUPPOSED TO DO ABOUT THAT, HUH?
TRY STUDYING..

BOY, DO I WISH PETER WAS THE ARTFUL DODGER...

SSSSKT
BUT HE'S NOT.
TEEN
CARROT STICKS AGAIN?
YOU'RE GOING TO TURN INTO A CARROT.
I WILL BE A SIZE FOUR BY THE DANCE.
THAT CAN'T BE HEALTHY.
SNAP

IT IS TOO.
SNAP
THE DIET'S IN THIS ISSUE OF *TEEN STYLE.*

IT SAYS EAT CARROTS FOR LUNCH THE FIRST DAY.
NOT FOR EVERY MEAL, EVERY DAY.

GIVE IT BACK.

NOPE! MY TURN!

BABE, YOU DON'T NEED THIS.
YOU'RE HOTT WITH TWO T'S.

LET'S PASS THIS ON...

FWAP
TEEN
...TO SOMEONE WHO REALLY NEEDS IT!
Merry Christmas, fashion failures!

MAN, JUST ONCE I'D LIKE TO MAKE IT THROUGH LUNCH WITHOUT BEING USED FOR TARGET PRACTICE.

PFFT!
New make up
"FIVE SURE-FIRE CRUSH STRATEGIES"...
"MAKEUP TECHNIQUES OF TEEN STARS"...
TEEN

IT'S LIKE THEY'RE PROGRAMMING US TO BE DUMB.

...

LET'S LOOK AT THE DRESSES.
OKAY.
New make up
TEEN

OOH, PRETTY!
HMM...
OH, SKIRT WAY TOO SHORT!

New
make t
TEEN

Sigh...
YOU'RE RIGHT.
I COULD ACTIVELY FEEL MY BRAIN CELLS COMMITTING SUICIDE WHILE READING THAT.
TEEN
FLOP

BESIDES, I DON'T EVEN HAVE ENOUGH MONEY FOR A MALL DRESS, MUCH LESS THE ONES IN THAT MAGAZINE.
What kind of teenager buys $500 dresses?
YEAH.
YEAH!

YEAH, FORGET THE MALL, WE'LL HIT THE SAM!
CLAP CLAP
HUH?
AFTER SCHOOL. THE SAMARITAN ARMY RESALE STORE IN TOWN.
ALL THE RICH LADIES TAKE THEIR OLD DRESSES DOWN TO THE SAMARITAN AFTER THEY'VE WORN THEM, LIKE, ONCE.
My mom does, too.
GOOD CALL!
SIGH...

SO, WHAT'S IT LIKE, HAVING TO SPEND AN HOUR WITH NERD QUEEN EVERY NIGHT?
...

THAT WAS KAT, OVER AT YOUR PLACE LAST NIGHT?
YEAH, I TOLD YOU.

NO, YOU JUST SAID YOU COULDN'T COME TO THE MOVIES WITH US.
YOU DIDN'T SAY WHY.

I THOUGHT IT WAS BECAUSE YOU HAD HEARD FROM NICK.
WHATEVER.

SO THE ARTFUL DODGER HAS TO BE SOMEONE WHO BENEFITS IF PRINCESS MARIE-LOUISE GETS SCARED OFF FROM COMING TO DOVER ACADEMY.
MENS-WEAR
KIDS-WEAR
THAT WOULD DEFINITELY BE CHLOE, BECAUSE THEN SHE STAYS QUEEN BEE.
BUT IT WOULD ALSO HAVE TO BE SOMEONE SMART, BECAUSE THE PRANKS ARE PRETTY CLEVER.
WHICH WOULD RULE CHLOE OUT.
MAYBE SHE'S ACTUALLY SUPER-INTELLIGENT, AND IT'S ALL SOME ELABORATE RUSE.

I DUNNO...
I DON'T THINK SHE HAD ENOUGH TIME AT THE ART MUSEUM TO STEAL THAT PAINTING AFTER MR. TEMPLAR BUSTED HER FOR SNEAKING OFF TO NEWBURY STREET.
CHANGING ROOMS
OR SHE'S HAVING SOMEONE ELSE DO THE DIRTY WORK--THE PERSON I SAW IN HER ROOM THAT NIGHT.
ACTUALLY, SPEAKING OF MR. TEMPLAR...

YOU GO FIRST.
OKAY, THANKS.
I LOOKED UP THE SCHOOL IN ANNAPOLIS THAT HE TAUGHT AT BEFORE.
STALKER.

I AM NOT!
...

Okay, maybe just a little bit.
BUT GET THIS. THERE'S NO RECORD OF HIM AT THAT SCHOOL.

IN FACT, THERE'S NO RECORD OF HIM ON THE ENTIRE INTERNET.

Y'KNOW, THAT DOESN'T AUTOMATICALLY MEAN ANYTHING SUSPICIOUS.
OH YES, IT DOES!
If you're not on the Internet, you don't exist!

DARN... I WAS COUNTING ON HIS HELP IN THE STING I'M SETTING UP TO CATCH THE ARTFUL DODGER.

CAN WE AGREE THAT, FOR NOW, HE GOES BACK TO "HOT NEW ART TEACHER"?
AND WE INVESTIGATE THE WHOLE "MAN THAT GOOGLE FORGOT" ANGLE NEXT SEMESTER?
OKAY.
But I'll keep following him, just in case.
HEY, THE PURPLE DRESS! YOU GOING TO SHOW ME IT?
NOPE!
COME ON...
IT LOOKS TERRIBLE.
I LOOK GROSS IN DRESSES.
SEE?

IT'S NOT TOO BAD...
BUT IT'S NOT GOOD, EITHER.
SIGH...
PFFT. ALL THOSE DRESSES, IN ALL THOSE STYLES...
...AND EVERY SINGLE ONE MAKES ME LOOK LIKE A TOAD.
YOUR TURN.

I THINK THERE'S SOMETHING WRONG WITH ME.
THERE'S NOTHING WRONG WITH YOU.
IT'S YOUR WORD AGAINST THE ENTIRE AMERICAN FASHION INDUSTRY, KAT.
FACE IT. AS A GIRL, I'M DEFECTIVE.
NONSENSE. AND IF IT'S ANY CONSOLATION...
...I'M NOT HAVING ANY LUCK EITHER.
I couldn't even zip up the green dress.
!

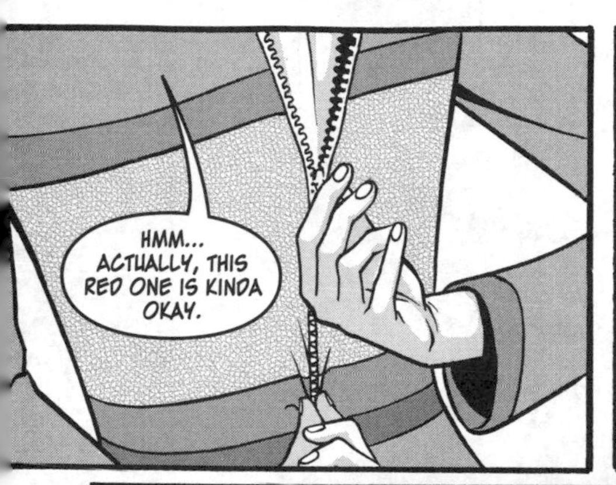
HMM... ACTUALLY, THIS RED ONE IS KINDA OKAY.

MOUSE, WHAT DO YOU THINK?

MOUSE?!

SORRY, I WAS TRYING SOMETHING ON.

CHECK IT OUT...

WOW!

YOU LOOK WICKED!
THIS IS GOING TO BE THE BEST DANCE EVER!

Chapter 4:
The Tempest
THE SAMARITAN ARMY
THE SAMARITAN ARMY

SNOW BALL 2007
I'LL PICK YOU UP AT 10.
YES, MOM.

BE ON TIME, BECAUSE I DON'T WANT TO HAVE TO COME IN AND FIND YOU.
NO, MOM.

THEY SAY THERE'S BAD WEATHER AHEAD.
TAKE MY MOBILE PHONE, IN CASE WE NEED TO COME GET YOU EARLY.
OKAY, MOM.

WAIT! ONE MORE THING...

YOU TWO LOOK BEAUTIFUL.
HAVE A GREAT TIME.

THANKS, MOM.

NICK!
DUDE! IT'S GREAT TO SEE YOU! WHERE YOU BEEN?
I TOOK A COUPLE DAYS OFF.
THINKING SOME STUFF THROUGH.
CHLOE!
YAY! YOU PASSED THE SCIENCE QUIZ!
Or did your dad un-ground you?
PASS? HA!
I GOT AN A-!
NICE ONE! I ALWAYS THOUGHT A GIRL WITH A PHOTOGRAPHIC MEMORY FOR EVERY CHRISTIAN LOUBOUTIN SHOE EVER SHOULD DO BETTER IN SCH--
--OOOOOO!

OHMIGOSH! I AM SO JEALOUS!
THEY'RE MY MOM'S.
SHE'S LETTING ME BORROW THEM FOR THE DANCE.
Sort of.
ROBE
YEAH, BAYBEE!
THE PARTY CAN START NOW!

NICK! YOU OKAY, DUDE?
HOW YOU DOIN'?
I'D BE BETTER IF EVERYONE STOPPED ASKING ME HOW I WAS.
HEY, PETER, I THOUGHT YOU WERE GROUNDED.

YEAH, SO?
I SNUCK OUT.
OOH...
SWEETIE! ARE YOU SICK?
NO, I'M FINE.
I'M A SIZE TWO.
HELLOOO, DOVER ACADEMY!

WELCOME TO THE 2007 SNOW BALL!
START HEADING DOWN TO THE DANCE FLOOR, BECAUSE I'M ABOUT TO DROP SOME HEAVENLY TUNES!
IN FIVE...

FOUR...
THREE...
TWO...
ONE...

MAY YOU LIVE IN INTERESTING TIMES...
OH NO...
KISS GOODNIGHT TO REASON, BUT NEVER RHYME...
CHLOE, THAT DRESS...

IT'S YOUR DRESS FROM LAST YEAR!
RESTROOMS
WARDROBE
NERD QUEEN IS WEARING YOUR OLD DRESS!
PEEL BACK THE SKIN FROM THE SKULL, WE'RE ALL GRINNING

ALL OF THE MEN, ALL OF THE WOMEN...
SHE MUST HAVE PICKED IT OUT OF THE TRASH WHEN SHE TUTORED YOU!
HA HA HA HA HA HA HA HA HA!

SHUT UP, YOU POISON DWARF!
WHY ARE YOU ONLY HAPPY WHEN YOU'RE MAKING OTHER PEOPLE MISERABLE?!
WHAT ARE YOU, MOUSE...
OOOH...
...HER BOYFRIEND?
I'M GONNA GO SIT DOWN FOR A SEC.

BECAUSE YOU'RE *DRESSED LIKE IT!*
COME ON, DUDE. LET'S GET A DRINK.
WHAT *IS* THIS SONG?
SHUT. UP.

YOU'RE NOT JUST FRIENDS!
I'M TELLIN' THE DJ TO PUT ON SOME SLIPKNOT.

YOU'RE *LESBI-FRIENDS!*
UH, MIMI...

SNAP
ACK!
HA HA HA HA HA HA HA!
HA HA HA HA HA HA HA!

HA HA! WHAT DO YOU THINK...
...GUYS?
GUYS?!
HELP!

THAT WAS "INTERESTING TIMES" BY EVIL GENIUS! WE'RE FOLLOWING THAT UP WITH OUTKAST'S NEWEST SINGLE...
PLEASE...
...DON'T HIT ME...
SKRUNCH

COME ON. SHE'S NOT WORTH IT.
BONK
WHAT'S GOING ON HERE?
...NOTHING.

IT'S OKAY...
DON'T LISTEN TO THAT WITCH... YOU LOOK AWESOME...
BAM

SOMEBODY STOLE MY NECKLACE!
KAT, YOU HAVE TO HELP ME!
WHAT?!
WE DON'T HAVE TO DO SQUAT FOR YOU.
GO TELL A TEACHER. THAT'S WHAT THEY'RE THERE FOR.
YOU DON'T UNDERSTAND!
MY MOM DOESN'T KNOW I BORROWED THE NECKLACE!

NO, YOU DON'T UNDERSTAND.
THE ONLY REASON YOU COULD COME TO THE DANCE IS BECAUSE I'VE SPENT THE WEEK TUTORING YOU.
BUT DID YOU STAND UP FOR ME OR MOUSE EARLIER?
NO, YOU DIDN'T.
I'M CALLING MY MOM, AND MOUSE AND I ARE GOING HOME.

FORGET YOU, FORGET YOUR STUPID NECKLACE, FORGET THIS STUPID DANCE...
...AND FORGET THIS INSANE SCHOOL. THIS ISN'T WORTH IT.
I'M SORRY... YOU DON'T KNOW HOW HARD IT IS...
NO.
NO.
I'M NOT GOING TO GIVE UP THAT EASILY.
YOU CAN'T GO AROUND DOING THIS TO PEOPLE.
YOU CAN'T LET BAD THINGS HAPPEN AND JUST TURN YOUR HEAD LIKE IT HAS NOTHING TO DO WITH YOU.

WE'LL FIND YOUR NECKLACE.
BECAUSE WE CAN.
BECAUSE NO MATTER HOW POPULAR YOU ARE...
...I NEVER WANT TO BE LIKE YOU.
To Be Concluded...

4 The Knave of Diamonds

In which a necklace is sought, a revenge enacted, a thief unmasked, and a teacher is found to possess many secrets. Chloe's diamond necklace has been stolen, and it will be up to Kat and Mouse to find it. But this mystery will have stunning ramifications that will shake Dover Academy to its very core. Everything changes when Kat & Mouse continues!

Try This at Home!

Want to turn common light into rainbows the way Kat and Chloe do in Chapter 2? You don't need a fancy prism– you can do it with a few basic items found in the kitchen!

You'll need:

- A small mirror (such as a makeup mirror)
- A piece of white paper or white card
- A glass jar or baking dish
- A flashlight
- A friend!

In art class, if you mix the seven colors of paint that correspond to the colors in a rainbow, you'll just get an ugly brown-black. But if you mix red, orange, yellow, green, blue, indigo and violet light, you get white! This is why "normal" light appears colorless.

However, when normal light is dispersed by such things as water, finely grooved reflective surfaces, or even a prism, this "breaks" the white light into its component wavelengths, each of which show up as a different, bright color.

To create your own homemade rainbow, find a place in your home with a sunny window. Fill a glass jar or a glass baking dish about half full with water. Put a mirror in the jar, angled slightly upward.

This experiment works best when the rest of the room is dark and the only light source is the sun coming in the window.

Next, turn the jar so the sunlight hits the part of the mirror that is underwater. Have your friend move the white paper or card around until it catches the light that bounces off the mirror – it will show up on the paper as a rainbow.

Now pull the shades down and turn on the flashlight. Shine the flashlight on the underwater part of the mirror, and get your friend to hold the card up to catch the refraction. Notice anything different about the colors that show up? Certain colors are more prominent in your flashlight-rainbow than in your sunlight-rainbow.

If you had a fluorescent light to shine on the submerged mirror, you'd notice that an even DIFFERENT set of colors was strongest. Not all white light is equal; each type of light source will have its own tint or "temperature." Movie directors and photographers spend much of their day dealing with issues of light's temperature, intensity and reflection, and what happens when light is bent through a curved glass lens.

You can also make a rainbow by shining a bright light on the bottom side of a music CD, or by spraying a garden hose on its finest setting up into the air on a sunny day.

KAT'S HEROES 3: ADA BYRON

The daughter of Lord Byron, the famous English poet, Ada Byron's parents separated when she was very young. Terrified that Ada would grow up to be wild like her father, Lady Byron encouraged Ada to study sensible, logical subjects like science and mathematics, rather than literature and poetry.

This was fortunate, as Ada showed a real gift for mathematics early in her life, and was tutored by famous mathematicians and scientists such as Mary Somerville and Augustus de Morgan. When she was 18 years old, Ada was introduced to another mathematician named Charles Babbage.

Babbage had created plans for an "Analytical Engine," a steam-powered calculating machine 30 meters long by 10 meters wide that was controlled by punched cards (a technique used with mechanical weaving looms of the time). It was--you guessed it--the first computer. Babbage spoke a lot about his Analytical Engine, but by the 1840s, he still hadn't written about it. The only account was written in a French journal by an Italian mathematician Babbage had met while traveling.

Ada had been interested in the Analytical Engine for over ten years, and understood it very well. Also, unlike Babbage, she spoke French, and she was asked to provide a translation of the French article for the British scientific community. She did so, adding extensive footnotes. Within her notes was a method, in complete detail, for using the machine to calculate a sequence of numbers known as Bernoulli numbers. This makes Ada a leading candidate for the title of world's first computer programmer!

For a woman who significantly advanced the field of mathematics, it was ironic that Ada's death came from medical ignorance. She was killed at 36, the same age as her father, and by the same technique: "medicinal bloodletting," thought at the time to cure disease. Her daughter, Lady Anne Blunt, became famous in her own right as a traveller in the Middle East.

MOUSE'S HEROES 3: VIVIENNE MALONE MAYES

Vivienne Malone Mayes was very smart, graduating from her high school at age 16 to go straight into the mathematics programme at Fisk University in Nashville. Vivienne studied under Evelyn Granville, the second black woman in the US to get her PhD in Mathematics. Inspired, Mayes decided to get a PhD herself. It was a 12-year struggle, and when she finally achieved it in 1966, she was still only the fifth black woman to receive one in Mathematics.

After seven years chairing the Math department at a small Texas college run by the African Methodist Episcopal Church, Mayes applied in 1962 for graduate school at Baylor, which was near her hometown. But the university rejected her, sending her a letter spelling out its segregation policy. Then she applied to University of Texas, which was being forced by federal law to desegregate at the time.

Vivenne Malone Mayes was the only black and the only woman in her first class. The other students wouldn't speak to her, falling silent if she walked over to them. Her advisor and classmates held their class discussions at a local coffeehouse that didn't serve blacks. The closest she could get to those discussions--crucial to success in the class--was hearing bits of conversation as her classmates passed her outside the café. Another professor, considered one of the leading Math teachers in America, wouldn't allow her to enroll in his class because he refused to teach blacks.

Despite all this, Vivienne got fantastic grades, and kept fighting toward her degree. She became seen as a model student.

Vivienne received her PhD in 1966 and then went back to Baylor--the very university that wouldn't let her in five years before--to teach. She remained at Baylor until she retired in 1994. She was lauded as an inspirational teacher of generations of students.